DERMACOMICS

A Fun Learning Journey into
Skin, Hair and Nail Care

Created by
Dr. Gitika Sanodia Biyani

Dedication

To my parents, who have always inspired me to explore, learn, and create.
To my teachers and seniors, whose guidance shaped my journey.
To my family, my husband, and my little ones, whose love and support make everything possible.

Table of Contents

Preface

Skincare can be confusing. With endless myths, trends, and misinformation floating around, understanding what truly works for your skin, hair, and nails can feel overwhelming. As a dermatologist, I've seen firsthand how common misconceptions lead to frustration, ineffective treatments, and even skin damage. This is why I created Dermacomics—a fun, easy-to-understand guide to help you navigate the world of skincare with confidence.

Through the character of Dr. Derma G, I aim to answer common skincare questions in a way that feels less like a lecture and more like a friendly conversation. Each chapter is designed to be interactive, insightful, and, most importantly, fun!

This book is a labor of love, inspired by my passion for dermatology and my desire to make skincare education accessible to all. I hope Dermacomics empowers you to make informed choices about your skin, hair, and nails and helps you embrace a healthier, more confident version of yourself.

Happy reading and happy skin!

Dr. Gitika A Biyani

Acknowledgments

Writing Dermacomics has been a journey filled with learning, creativity, and passion. This book wouldn't have been possible without the encouragement and support of so many wonderful people.

First and foremost, I express my deepest gratitude to my parents, who have always inspired me to think beyond the ordinary and strive for excellence. Their unwavering belief in me has been my greatest strength.

To my teachers and seniors, thank you for your invaluable guidance, mentorship, and for instilling in me the knowledge and skills that I bring to this book. Your lessons continue to shape my journey in dermatology and beyond.
Thank you to Paridhi and Shivangi for their constant support in designing this book

To my family and husband Ankit , thank you for your endless patience, love, and support throughout this process. Your belief in my vision has kept me motivated, even on the toughest days.

And finally, to my beautiful daughters, Arya and Ruhi, whose laughter, love, and innocence bring boundless joy to my life. You are my biggest inspiration.
This book is a labor of love, and I hope it helps many in their skincare journey.

Dermacomics

The Fun Guide to Skin, Hair & Nail Care

About the Book:

Dermacomics is an engaging and informative guide to skin, hair, and nail care, presented in a fun, comic-style format. This book simplifies complex dermatological concepts, making skincare education accessible and enjoyable for everyone. Whether you're struggling with acne, confused about your skin type, or looking for practical hair and nail care tips, Dermacomics has got you covered!

CHAPTER: 1
WHATS YOUR SKIN TYPE?

Everyone's skin has its own quirks! Whether you're team 'Oily', 'Dry', 'Combo', or 'Sensitive,' there's a routine just for you.
Olivia Oil
Diana Dry
Carl Combo
Sam Sensitive

Oil Free
Hey, Doc! this shine is driving me crazy! By noon, my face is super oily, and I keep blotting and powdering, but it just won't go away
That excess oil can be tricky to manage. stick with oil-free, non-comedogenic products, so they won't clog your pores. Also, gentle exfoliation a couple of times a week will help control that oil build-up without over-stripping your skin.

Oh, Diana, dry skin can definitely be a challenge. For you, I recommend focusing on hydrating cleansers that won't strip your skin. After that, a rich, creamy moisturizer will lock in hydration. Avoid harsh soaps
Hi Dr I'm Diana ,My skin feels tight and uncomfortable, especially when it's cold. Sometimes it even flakes.
Dry Skin Products
CREAM
CREAM

FOR DRY SKIN
Hey, Doc! I'm Carl Combo. My T-zone is all oily, but my cheeks are dry and flaky. I'm constantly switching between blotting and moisturizing, and I'm never sure what to do!
That's a classic combo skin dilemma, Carl! For you, a balanced routine is key. Use a gentle, non-stripping cleanser that won't over-dry or over-oil your skin. Then, try applying a lightweight moisturizer on your T-zone and a richer cream on your cheeks.

Sensitive skin needs gentle handling. Stick with fragrance-free, hypoallergenic products. And before using anything new, always patch-test on a small area first to ensure your skin doesn't react.
Hello, Dr. Derma. I'm Sam Sensitive. My skin is super reactive—one wrong product, and I'm red and itchy for days.

Remember, everyone's skin is different. Embrace yours, and take care of it with the right routine!
Olivia Oil
Diana Dry
Carl Combo
Sam Sensitive

CHAPTER: 2
TRUTH ABOUT ACNE

Myth Busting
Cleansing Frequency
Over-cleansing can actually irritate your skin and make acne worse! Stick to a gentle cleanse twice a day
Moisturizer for Oily Skin
Even oily skin needs moisture! Skipping moisturizer can actually make your skin produce more oil. Choose a lightweight, oil-free one instead.
Popping Pimples
Popping pimples can push bacteria deeper into the skin, causing more inflammation. Hands off for healthier skin!

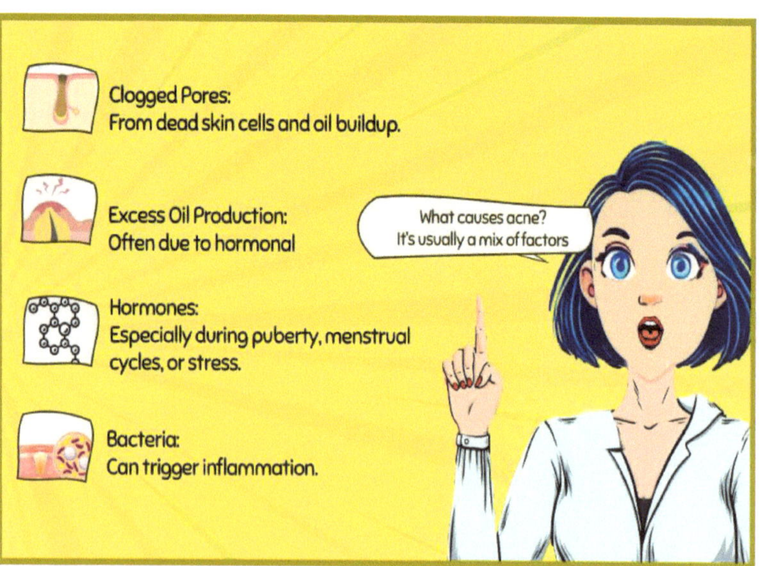

Acne comes in different forms. Here's the lowdown

Blackheads
Open pores clogged with sebum

Whiteheads
Closed pores with a white bump

Pustules
Inflamed bumps filled with pus

Cystic Acne
Deep, painful lumps under the skin

Clogged Pores:
From dead skin cells and oil buildup.

Excess Oil Production:
Often due to hormonal

Hormones:
Especially during puberty, menstrual cycles, or stress.

Bacteria:
Can trigger inflammation.

What causes acne?
It's usually a mix of factors

Helps unclog pores.
Reduces bacteria and inflammation.
Promote cell turnover and reduce acne formation.
Acne isn't a one-size-fits-all situation. Here are a few treatments that can help
Salicylic Acid
Benzoyl Peroxide
RETINOL
Remember, acne care takes time and consistency. Be gentle, avoid picking, and talk to a dermatologist if you need help!

CHAPTER: 3
SENSITIVE SKINCARE: DO'S AND DONT'S

Always patch test on your arm before using new products on your face. It's a quick and easy way to prevent irritation
TONER

Avoid gritty scrubs! Harsh exfoliants can damage sensitive skin. Go for a mild chemical exfoliant instead.
NO
SCRUB

Fragrance free skincare

Sensitive skin can easily be overwhelmed. Keep it simple a gentle cleanser, moisturizer, and SPF are all you need.
Opt for moisturizers with soothing ingredients, like aloe or chamomile, to hydrate and calm your skin.

Sensitive skin needs sun protection too! Go for mineral sunscreens with zinc oxide or titanium dioxide for gentle coverage.

With sensitive skin, less is often more
Stick to gentle
minimal routines
let your skin adjust at its own pace.

CHAPTER: 4
HAIRCARE BASICS

There are many reasons for hair fall. It can happen naturally during the telogen phase, after illness like a viral infection, or even due to a lack of essential vitamins. Let's look into what might be affecting you.
My scalp is itchy, and I'm noticing more hair fall. What could be the reason?

Hair care Unit
What causes dandruff, and why am I also losing more hair?
- Dandruff can come from a dry scalp, buildup, or fungal infections.
- Hair fall can be due to natural shedding phases, recent illness, or vitamin deficiencies.
- Understanding these can help us find the right care routine for you.

Washing too frequently can strip your scalp of natural oils. For most people, washing 2–3 times a week is ideal.

For a healthy scalp, look for ingredients like tea tree oil to reduce dandruff, and aloe vera to soothe.

Heavy styling products can cause buildup and clog hair follicles. Use them sparingly for healthier hair.
VOLUME SPRAY
SUPER STRONG
SUPER VOLUME
STYLING CREAM
MAGIC MIST
HAIR GEL

Scalp massage increases blood flow and can help reduce stress, which benefits both your scalp and hair.

Healthy hair care is about balance. Keep it simple, choose products wisely, and enjoy your scalp care routine
Wash 2-3 times weekly
Choose gentle products
Massage regularly

When stress strikes, take a moment to pause, breathe deeply, and do something that brings you joy. Your skin—and mind—will thank you!
stress-relief
CHECK LIST
Take breaks
Breathe deeply
Connect with loved ones

CHAPTER: 5
NAILCARE BASICS

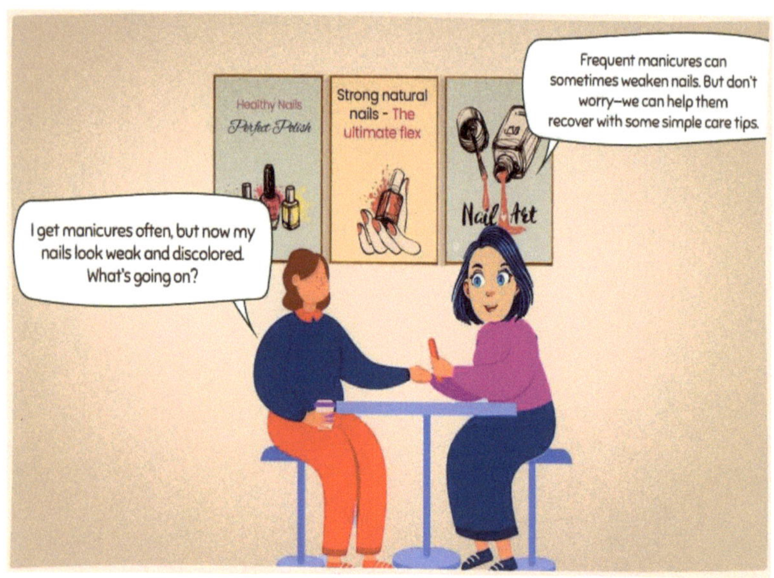

Healthy Nails
Perfect Polish
Strong natural nails - The ultimate flex
Nail Art
Frequent manicures can sometimes weaken nails. But don't worry—we can help them recover with some simple care tips.
I get manicures often, but now my nails look weak and discolored. What's going on?

Your nails have multiple layers that need care. A balanced diet with vitamins like biotin and zinc keeps them strong from within.
Biotin and vitamin rich food
nail plate
nail bed
cuticle

Cuticles are a natural barrier against infection. Avoid cutting them—instead, keep them moisturized with cuticle oil and gently push them back.
Look for acetone-free polish removers and strengthening polishes. These products are gentler on nails and help prevent damage over time.
Acetone Free Strengthening Formula

Fungal infections thrive in damp environments. Keep your nails clean and dry, avoid sharing nail tools, and consider using antifungal treatments if needed.
Antifungal cream
HEALTHY NAIL
FUNGAL INFECTION

Nails need time to breathe. Going polish-free for a few days every month helps them recover and prevents discoloration and brittleness.

Biting or peeling nails weakens them and increases the risk of infection. Break these habits to keep nails healthy and strong.
NO

CHAPTER: 6
STRESS AND YOUR SKIN

When you're stressed, your body releases cortisol, a hormone that can trigger breakouts and make your skin feel dry. But don't worry, thereare ways to manage it!

Stress increases inflammation and oil production, which can clog pores and cause redness. Taking care of your mind can help keep your skin clear.

Simple self-care practices like deep breathing, meditation, and regular exercise can help reduce stress and support healthier skin.
Exercise
Meditation

Mindful skincare is about being gentle. Opt for calming products, like a soothing cleanser and hydrating moisturizer, to keep skin balanced during stressful times.

Sleep is your skin's best friend! Aim for 7-8 hours to let your skin recover and reduce stress.
Stay hydrated and eat nutrient-rich foods. Water and a balanced diet are essential to combatting the effects of stress on your skin.
Stay hydrated
Eat balanced diet
When stress strikes, take a moment to pause, breathe deeply, and do something that brings you joy. Your skin—and mind—will thank you!
stress-relief
CHECK LIST
Take breaks
Breathe deeply
Connect with loved ones

<u>Epilogue</u>

Beyond the pages your Skin,Hair and Nail care journey continues

As we reach the end of Dermacomics, I hope this journey has helped you understand basics of your skin, hair, and nails better—while making learning fun along the way! Skincare isn't just about products and treatments; it's about understanding your body, making informed choices, and embracing self-care with confidence.

Through the pages of this book, I aimed to simplify complex dermatological concepts and clear up common myths, all while keeping things engaging and relatable. But remember, skincare is not one-size-fits-all—it's a lifelong process of learning and adapting to your skin's changing needs.